MURDER AT THE HAUNTED HOUSE

HAWK THERIOT & KRISTI BLOCKER SHORT
STORIES BOOK 1

JIM RILEY

To the most beautifully

You always have been and always will be

1

LIGHTNING FLASHED AHEAD. THUNDER FOLLOWED. RAIN drops pelted the two identical girls.

The Thomas twins crept toward the creaky old homestead like a mouse trying to sneak past a house cat. The shining moon cast ominous shadows through the moss-laden live oak trees over the wooden frame at the edge of the swamp. A night owl hooted from a lower limb.

"Are you sure we should be doing this?" Mandy asked.

Mindy grabbed her sister's hand. "Duh. If we want to meet a ghost, we have to go where the ghosts are."

"Couldn't we throw a ghost party and send out invitations?"

"C'mon, Mandy. If we knew where to send the invitations we wouldn't be wandering around in the dark on a damp night. Sometimes you don't make much sense."

"This place is spooky." Mandy shuddered.

"Silly. If it wasn't spooky, there wouldn't be any ghosts here."

"Okay, but you're going in first."

Mindy climbed the squeaky steps to reach the front door and carefully turned the door knob.

"It's open. I told you ghosts don't need to lock their doors."

Mandy remained a step behind her sister, holding onto the back of her belt to support her shaky legs.

"You also told me they were cute and cuddly. This doesn't feel cute and cuddly to me."

"Hush. Where's the light switch?"

"There's not any electricity in here. It's been turned off forever."

Mindy sighed, "Then how do the ghosts cook their dinner?"

"I don't know. What do ghosts eat anyway?"

"Beats me. We'll have to ask Hawk. He knows everything."

"No, he doesn't know everything."

"What is it he doesn't know?"

Mandy giggled, "He doesn't know how to get Kristi to marry him. They've been engaged forever and they're still not married. If I was her, I'd dump him."

Mindy sighed, "I wouldn't. He's too cute to dump. She might try fishing in another lake, but I wouldn't throw him back in."

"You just want him for yourself."

"Do not. He's too—he's too—"

Mandy laughed. "The only thing he's too much of for you is engaged."

Mindy pulled ahead. "We're supposed to be looking for ghosts, not talking about Hawk."

Mandy tried to peer up the rickety stairs.

"Don't ghosts usually hang out upstairs? We should've brought a flashlight so we could see."

Mindy shook her head, tossing her long strawberry-blonde hair from side to side.

"We couldn't do that. Light scares away the ghosts. They'd never come out if we came in here shining flashlights all over the place."

"That'd be okay with me. I'm not sure this was a very good idea."

"Sure it is. All of our ideas are good. Some just don't work out like we planned." Mindy exuded confidence.

"Hold on. Don't go so fast. One of these old steps might give way on us."

"If we don't go up them, we won't find any ghosts and the whole night will be wasted."

"I'd rather waste the night than break a leg. You're going too fast. We need to sneak up on them."

"I bet they already know we're here. Ghosts can hear everything. Don't you know anything about ghosts?"

"I know to stay away from 'em."

Mindy led Mandy up the stairs to the loft overlooking the first floor. A railing ran the entire length of the loft.

Mindy looked back at her sister.

"Be careful hanging onto this railing. I don't know how sturdy it is."

"Don't worry. I'm hanging onto you. As long as you're here, I'm okay. Why are we whispering?"

"Because ghosts like quiet places. That's why they hang out at cemeteries. People there don't say much at night."

The sisters crept about half the length of the rail in the darkness, feeling their way along.

"Oops, what is it?" Mindy exclaimed in the darkness.

"What is what?" Mandy asked.

"I bumped into something lying on the floor. I can't see what it is."

"I don't see it."

"Wait a second. I'll check it out." Mindy whispered.

Mindy bent over and felt the lump with one hand and holding onto her sister with the other one. She felt a handle coming out of the lump and pulled on it. The object came out of the lump with surprising ease. She held it up so the moonlight barely glimmering through the window could illuminate it.

Mindy shrieked. "Oh my God! It's a knife!"

"Are you sure?"

Mindy's voice was shaken and uneven. "And there's the body it was in. Let's get out of here."

Mindy rose and took a step back toward the stairs. Suddenly a bright beam of light encircled them from the lower floor. The twins tried to shield their eyes from the glare.

"What are you doing up there?" The voice was loud and gruff.

"Nothing." Mindy answered before she looked down and realized she was still holding the knife dripping with blood.

2

"I FOUND THEM STANDING OVER MY GRANDFATHER'S BODY with the knife still in their hands, Sheriff. What more could you want?" Brent Atkins pointed at the twins.

Sheriff Kristi Cates picked up the clear evidence bag containing the wet knife. Then she turned her attention to Mindy and Mandy sitting in the chairs on the other side of the conference table.

"What were ya'll doing there tonight?"

Mandy glanced at Mindy before speaking.

"Just looking for ghosts, Kristi. We didn't have time to find any before I tripped over Mr. Atkins body."

Kristi shook her head. "Ya'll were looking for ghosts at that old shack?"

"It's the only place in town other than the cemetery that has any."

Kristi looked down at the floor and closed her eyes. Then she turned her attention to Brent.

"What was your grandfather doing there tonight?"

"Gramps lived there his whole life. At least until he couldn't take care of it himself any longer. Then he moved in with me and my wife. Mom and Dad died two years ago in a wreck on Highway 90 and my brothers and I are the only family he has left. He moved in with us because we don't have kids and have more room than my brothers. After Gramps moved out, the old house got the reputation of being haunted and a lot of the kids from town thought it was cool to go there."

He cast an accusatory glance at the twins.

"Gramps liked to go by the place and make sure there weren't any kids there tearing up his house. That's what he was doing there tonight."

"And why were you there, Brent?"

"Gramps had been gone for a while. It's only a short walk from my house to his old place. He should've returned a lot earlier. He didn't so I went over there to make sure he hadn't fallen or something."

"And what happened once you got there?"

"I walked in and heard a noise up above me. When I shined the light up there, I saw one of the girls holding a knife in her hand. I don't know which one. I can't tell them apart."

Kristi looked back at the twins.

"Is that what happened, girls?"

"That's right as far as what he said. I was the one holding the knife. But I didn't know it was a knife when I grabbed it. I promise." Mindy looked pleadingly at Kristi.

"You girls are in big trouble. Do you want me to call your father?"

The twins looked at each other and nodded at the silent communication between them.

Mindy addressed Kristi, "We'd rather you call Hawk. He'll know what to do."

3

"How DID THE TWINS GET INTO THIS KIND OF MESS?" asked Hawk.

Kristi shook her head. "You know the twins as well as I do. They can get into some situations most people would never dream of, but to them it's normal. You'd think at almost twenty years old, they'd know better."

"I don't think with the twins' age is a determining factor. But why did they ask for me? I'm a federal ranger, not a lawyer."

Kristi laughed. "You know they think you can do anything. They didn't even consider calling their dad, which most young ladies would have done. Besides, I think at least one of them has a crush on you."

"I don't know, Kristi. This is serious. They'd be a lot better off with a lawyer than with me. If their lawyer thinks I can help, I'd be more than glad to do it."

Kristi looked directly into his eyes.

"Do it for me if you won't do it for them. They need you right now."

Hawk tried to look away from her clear blue eyes, but wasn't able to. He knew he couldn't refuse his fiancée.

"Alright, but if I find they did something silly, I'm gonna to bring it to you."

"The twins do something silly? Now that would be news." She laughed.

Hawk chuckled. "I guess you're right. What I meant is if they did do something to cause Mr. Atkins's death, which I don't believe they would ever intentionally do, then I'm going to have to report it."

"That's why I've made a special arrangement with the District Attorney. She trusts you too."

"What kind of arrangement?" He asked warily.

"I don't want to arrest them despite all of the evidence against them. So I came to an agreement with the DA. If they stay in your care, they won't have to go to jail."

"My care? Do you mean stay out at the camp with me? You've already made the arrangements, haven't you?"

Kristi grinned. "I knew you'd say yes. After all, they are the twins and I know how much you like them."

"Gee whiz, Kristi. Those girls are—are—"

"I know. They're a nuisance. But I think they're innocent. I just don't have the facts on my side. That's why I agree with them. You're the right man for the job."

"Huh? I'm not sure there is a right man to deal with the twins." Hawk paused. "But tell them I'll try to help them."

"They're already on their way to your camp," Kristi giggled.

4

Hawk smiled at the attractive lady in the upscale pants suit.

"Mrs. Atkins, is Brent in?"

"He should be back in a few minutes. May I help you?" She asked politely.

"I'm Hawk Theriot. I'm investigating the death of Brent's grandfather."

She cast an attractive smile at Hawk.

"Come on in. I'll put on some coffee while you wait for him. I know he wants to get this out of the way as quickly as possible."

"Thank you. I appreciate it."

Hawk entered the modern house in one of the nicer neighborhoods of Morgan City. He immediately admired the rich décor and the ornate furnishings. Glancing around the huge room, he looked at the mid-twenties woman.

"This is very nice, Mrs. Atkins."

"Please call me Sarah. Brent and I aren't that formal."

"Alright, Sarah. Brent told the sheriff his grandfather was living with you guys."

"That's correct. He's been—or was here for a couple of years. Would you like to see his room?"

"Certainly."

Hawk was not expecting to find anything of value in the old man's room, but had nothing else to do while waiting for Brent to show up. He followed Sarah through a series of halls to a large suite segregated from the rest of the house.

"This was Gramps's room. He could do his thing without us disturbing him."

Hawk looked around the room in amazement.

"He liked knives, didn't he?"

"He was a big collector," Sarah laughed. "All kinds of knives from the big to the little. He even has a few swords as part of his collection. Gramps had a fascination with them and once he discovered the internet, he couldn't control himself."

"He's got a bunch of them." Hawk scanned the room. "That's for sure."

Sarah smiled with a twinkle in her eye. "You haven't seen all of them. He has thousands stored around here in various rooms. I don't even think he knew how many he had. I don't know what we're going to do with them now."

"I'm sure you won't have any trouble getting rid of them. Knives are big business these days."

"I'm not sure Brent wants to sell them. They meant a lot to Gramps. And to think he was killed by one of his own knives by those two girls is just too much for me to think about."

Hawk shook his head. "I don't believe the girls—"

Sarah turned her head toward the front of the house. "I hear Brent. The coffee should be ready. Why don't we get some and you can talk to Brent?"

Hawk followed Sarah back through the maze of hallways

and sat down at the kitchen bar while she met her husband at the door. The couple returned to the kitchen.

"Hello, I'm Brent Atkins."

Hawk whistled under his breath at the thousand dollar pin-striped suit Brent was wearing.

"Brent, nice to meet you. Sorry to hear about the death of your grandfather. I'm Hawk Theriot."

"Are you with the Sheriff's Office?"

"I'm a federal investigator."

Brent frowned. "Federal? Why are you involved in my grandfather's death? He was killed by a couple of local girls."

"The Sheriff asked me to help out and see what I could find. Do you mind telling me what happened the night of his death?"

Brent recounted the Kristie story he had told Kristi according to the reports Hawk read. He followed the narration with the notes he'd brought with him. There was little variation between the accounts. When he finished, Hawk asked some of the questions not answered in the report.

"How often did your grandfather go to his house?"

"Probably once a week or so. It bothered him that it was getting rundown and all of the kids in town thought it was a freaky place."

"Why didn't he sell it?"

Brent shrugged. "Gramps always thought his health would improve enough and he'd get to move back there one day. He knew he was interfering with our lifestyle somewhat and that bothered him. He didn't want to be a burden on us."

"Was he?"

"Not really. We weren't able to go on trips like we had before we moved in because Sarah had to be here to cook and clean for him. He wasn't able to cook for himself anymore.

But he mostly stayed in his room and played with his knives. He has a huge collection."

Hawk nodded toward Sarah.

"She showed them to me. Unbelievable. What are you going to do with all of those?"

"I don't know. There's thousands of them. Even Gramps couldn't keep up with all he had. We may sell them and donate the proceeds to a charity or we may give them to someone. He might have left them to Marshall in his will. I don't want them. I didn't share my Gramps's passion for them."

"Did your grandfather have any enemies? Anybody that would want to do him harm?"

"Not that I know of. He pretty much stayed in his room most of the time. Sometimes my brothers would come by and take him to eat with them or go out."

"I saw in the report you have two brothers living here in Morgan City."

"Marshall and Dwayne. They both live here. Our parents are no longer living."

Hawk checked his notes once more. "I saw that in the report also. Sorry to hear. Are Marshall and Bill the only other relatives?"

"Yes."

"What kind of relationship did they have with your grandfather?"

"Marshall had a great relationship with him. He shared the same interest in knives Gramps had. I guess I should give the collection to him now that I think about it. Marshall would love to get his hands on all of them."

"How about Dwayne?"

"He didn't care about knives at all."

"I meant about the relationship between him and his grandfather. How was it?"

"Not very good. Gramps was always trying to get Dwayne to change his way of living. Dwayne likes to gamble a little bit and is always short of money. Gramps would give him some money and Dwayne would promise not to gamble anymore. It never worked out. Dwayne can't stay away from the gambling boats."

"Was Mr. Atkins wealthy?"

"I don't know if wealthy is the right word. His estate will be worth somewhere in the two million dollar range."

Hawk chuckled. "That's wealthy where I come from. Who inherits the estate?"

Bruce paused before answering. "As far as I know, it will be split evenly between the three of us boys. At least that was the way the will read the last time I saw it. That was before he moved in with us. He could have changed it since."

"Can you think of anyone who wanted to hurt your grandfather or had a grudge against him?"

"The neighbor on the east side gets upset when the lawn service doesn't keep the yard immaculate or the kids make too much noise at night. He thinks the old house is driving down the value of the other houses in the neighborhood. He and Gramps didn't get along real well when Gramps was living there, so I think most of it is a carryover from then."

"Do you know the neighbor's name?"

"It's Ira. Ira Stephens."

"Can I get the addresses and phone numbers for Marshall and Dwayne? I'd like to check with them to see if they know anything."

"No problem."

"Brent, for the record, did anyone see what time you left to search for your grandfather?"

"My wife can." He paused. "Uh— no, she may not be able to verify the exact time."

"Why would she not be able?"

"My wife sings in the choir at church. Sometimes the Minister of Music asks her to sing a solo for the special music. When he does, she locks herself in our music room hours at a time listening to different songs before choosing one. We had it sound-proofed and she can't hear much outside the room when she's in it. She was in the music room when I left and I didn't want to disturb her."

"So no one can truly verify when you left?"

"There isn't anyone. But what I told the Sheriff is exactly what happened. If you're insinuating I had something to do with Gramps's death, you're wrong."

"Don't get upset, Brent. I have to ask all the questions and see where the evidence leads. It's way too early for me to point any fingers at anyone."

5

HAWK STARED AT THE TWINS SITTING ON THE LOVE SEAT in the game room at the camp.

"Mindy, what were you guys thinking?" Hawk asked sternly.

"Detective Ranger, we just wanted to find a ghost. Everybody we know has seen one, but we haven't. It's our turn."

"Who do you know that's truly seen a ghost?"

"Almost everybody." Mindy hesitated. "At least most of the kids we know."

Hawk didn't say anything, but continued to stare at Mindy.

"One guy at work told us he has seen one. We believe him."

"Where did he see this ghost?"

Mindy paused. "Well, it wasn't actually him. His cousin's girlfriend's brother saw it."

Hawk rolled his eyes.

Mandy jumped in. "But we know it's true."

"And how do you know it's true?"

Mindy slapped her forehead. "Duh. If it wasn't true, he

wouldn't have told us. Boy, you don't think sometimes, do you?"

Hawk glanced up at the ceiling.

"I guess not. Luckily, I have you two to help me."

Mindy beamed. "That's what we're here for, Detective Ranger. You can always count on us."

6

Hawk was seated in the leather chair in the neat den of Marshall Atkins.

"Marshall, I'm sorry to hear about your grandfather. Your brother told me you and he shared a passion for knives."

The well dressed young man smiled. "We spent many hours together talking about them. We even compared collections."

Hawk chuckled. "Who had the best one?"

Marshall's smile broadened. "No doubt, he did. He spent all day on the computer and lots of money building his. I didn't have his time or his money."

"What kind of knives was he most interested? Hunting knives, military knives, display knives—?"

"He loved the antler knives. You know the ones where the handle is made from a deer's horns. If he had a favorite one, I would say that would be it. He had a collection to die for."

"Apparently."

"I didn't mean it like you heard it," Marshall held up his hand. "All I meant is he had great collection that anyone would be proud to own."

Hawk watched Marshall closely for any signs of deception.

"What's gonna happen to his knife collection now?"

"He always told me he'd leave it to me in his will. I honestly don't know if he did or not."

"Will the inheritance, if it works out that way cause any friction with your brothers?"

Marshall paused for more than a minute before answering.

"Gramps had some peculiar thoughts on life and death. I wouldn't be surprised to see a lot of friction when the estate is disbursed."

"What do ya mean?"

"Gramps didn't like Dwayne's style of living."

"You mean the gambling?"

"Gambling was part of it. He also didn't appreciate the girls, the expensive cars and all the other things in Dwayne's life he couldn't afford."

"I understand from Brent your grandfather bailed Dwayne out several times when Dwayne lost at the casinos."

"On more than a few occasions, to be sure."

"Do you have any idea what Dwayne's finances are like now?"

Marshall laughed out loud. "I imagine they're the same as always."

"And that would be?"

"My guess, and I would be extremely surprised if I'm wrong, is Dwayne has less than a hundred dollars in the bank and owes various bookies along the coast several thousand."

"Do you know any of his bookies?"

"I don't know any of them. I do know Gramps met with one of them and told him to quit taking bets from Dwayne.

Gramps used to have a lot of influence on the Gulf coast, but that was a long time ago."

"What does Dwayne do for a living?"

"Up until two days ago, he sponged off of Gramps. He couldn't hold down a job because of his drinking and late nights. Most employers don't appreciate an employee who only shows up for work two or three days a week."

Hawk chuckled.

"I can understand that."

"Gramps was getting tired of it though. The last time I got with him and talked about his newest knives, he told me it was the end of supporting Dwayne. He was tired of all of Dwayne's promises to quit gambling."

"What will Dwayne do now? He can't depend on his grandfather to bail him out any more."

"He's gonna go through whatever inheritance he gets like Sherman went through Atlanta. Then he's gonna be in a bind. But then, he might have been already if Gramps did cut him off."

"Is there anyone who would know if your grandfather cut the funds off?"

"Only Dwayne and Gramps. Maybe one of Dwayne's girlfriends, but he goes through them so often I quit trying to keep up."

"What do you know about your grandfather's relationship with Brent?"

"They got along splendidly. Gramps loved Brent and respected him. Brent returned the respect. As you obviously know, Brent let Gramps live with him after he could no longer take care of the house."

"So, as far as you know, there were no problems between them."

"I didn't say that."

"I'm sorry. I thought you told me they loved and respected each other."

"It's true. They did, but Brent also felt like he was tied down because of Gramps. Brent and his wife, Sarah, love to travel. Since Gramps moved in with them, I don't think they've been on a single trip. Brent felt obligated to stay there with Gramps."

"Why didn't they take your grandfather with them?"

"Like I told you, Gramps had some peculiar notions. He thought taking trips to faraway places was a waste of time and money. He always said we had the most beautiful marshes and the greenest forests right here in Louisiana and he couldn't imagine any other place in the world being any better."

"I can see where those ideas might conflict." Hawk smiled.

"Poor Brent was catching it from both sides. His wife was on one side and Gramps was on the other. Brent couldn't win no matter what he decided."

"Sounds like it. I wouldn't have wanted to be the referee between the two."

"Neither did Brent. I know he loved Gramps, but I'm also sure there's a little less tension around his house right now. The burden of taking care of an elderly relative can be overwhelming at times. My wife and I will always be grateful to Brent for taking Gramps in with them."

"Just so I don't have to come back to ask, where were you when your grandfather was killed?"

"Let's see. Brent found the girls there around ten, didn't he?"

"A little after ten."

"Unfortunately, I was home by myself. My wife decided to take the kids to a late movie and they didn't return until

MURDER AT THE HAUNTED HOUSE

after eleven. I didn't want to go to the movies. I stayed at home by myself and watched TV."

"Did anyone come by or did you call anyone that can verify you were home all night?"

"It was just me, the TV and my chocolate Lab. I haven't trained him to speak English yet."

7

HAWK EYED THE STUBBLE-FACED MAN IN THE WRINKLED clothes that smelled of tobacco and alcohol.

"Dwayne, thanks for seeing me."

"You're welcome. I heard you were asking questions about Gramps's death. What can I do for you?"

"I'd like to ask you about your grandfather."

Dwayne took a sip from the glass of brown liquid.

"I don't see how anything I know will help you, but come on in."

Hawk sat in one of the three chairs in the sparsely decorated den. It's covering was torn and dirty and one leg was shorter than the other three. The walls were unadorned and a moldy smell permeated throughout the room.

Dwayne was fidgeting in his chair.

"Is this going to take long? I have an appointment I need to go to soon."

"No problem. I'll hurry as fast as I can."

"Ask away."

"First, I'd like to get some background information on you?"

Dwayne took another swig.

"Why? Gramps died, not me."

"Just so we can be thorough in our investigation. You don't mind answering a few questions about yourself, do you?"

The dingy man hesitated before answering. "I suppose not."

"What is your occupation?"

Dwayne paused. "I'm a consultant."

"What area of consulting?"

"You could call it financial."

Hawk stared at the disheveled across from him.

"It's not about what I would call it. It's about what you do for a living."

"Okay. I'm a financial consultant."

"Who are your clients?"

"They vary."

"Where's your office?"

Dwayne looked around the sparse room. "I work out of my home. I'm an independent consultant."

"Is that how you support yourself?"

"I manage to get by."

Hawk pulled out a sheet of papers.

"According to the IRS, you made less than five thousand dollars last year. Are you sure consulting was your primary source of income?"

Dwayne slumped even more in his chair. "You've already talked to my brothers, haven't you?

Hawk nodded.

"So you know I sometimes bet a nickel or two. I got lucky last year and made some decent money on the games."

"According to your grandfather's records, you didn't do so well on the games either."

"What? You've looked at Gramps's bank account?"

"We try to complete a thorough investigation as I told you earlier."

"But digging through his records like that. Is that legal?"

"I assure you it's legal. Just as my background check on you was legal."

Dwayne slumped in his chair.

"So you know I'm not a financial consultant."

Hawk nodded. "I am aware of that, yes."

"So why didn't you tell me?"

"Sometimes it's best in an interview to let the other person speak."

"I wish you would've said something. Now, I'm gonna be late for my appointment."

"I'm sure they'll wait. Why don't we start over? What do you do for a living?"

Dwayne sighed. "I gamble. I bet on football games, basketball games and I go to the casinos on occasion."

"How much did you make last year gambling?"

"Look." Dwayne threw his hands in the air. "I had a streak of bad luck. I'm just about to break out of it."

"With your share of your grandfather's estate?"

"I don't need my grandfather's money," Dwayne glared at Hawk. "I'm doing pretty well by myself."

Hawk looked down at his notes. "Not according to his records, you're not."

"Then his records must be wrong."

"You must've forgotten. He made you sign an IOU for every dollar you borrowed. In the last year alone, you received almost two hundred thousand dollars from him."

Dwayne emptied his glass.

"I didn't borrow nearly that much from him. You gotta be mistaken."

Hawk held up the notes he'd brought.

"Would you like to see the receipts with your signature on them?"

Dwayne dropped his gaze to the floor.

"It didn't seem like two hundred thousand." He said dismally.

"How much do you owe now?"

Dwayne checked his empty glass. "Somewhere around twenty grand."

"Did you grandfather cut you off? Was he no longer supporting your gambling habits?"

"It wasn't like that. Sometimes Gramps was a little slow to come around, but he always did before it got too bad."

"Only this time he was serious. Is that right?"

Dwayne shook his head. "He was taking longer than usual. But he would've come up with the money soon."

"And if he didn't, what were you gonna do?"

"I didn't have to worry. He always came through."

"How much do you think you'll inherit?"

Dwayne shrugged. "I don't know. Gramps didn't share his financial standing with me. He might have told Brent."

"But you do know it would have been enough to get you out of your current financial bind, don't you?"

"I'm sure his estate would cover the little bit I owe," Dwayne nodded. "But I didn't kill my grandfather no matter how much money he had."

"So where were you the night your grandfather died?"

"I was entertaining a friend here at the house."

"Does your friend have a name?"

Dwayne stood and grabbed a bottle from the shelf behind him.

"I'm sure she does. But I don't remember it."

"How can I get in touch with your friend?"

"She didn't exactly leave me her phone number, if you know what I mean?"

"I can guess."

Dwayne sat back down and looked up at the ceiling.

"I don't even remember where I picked her up at."

"So you really don't have an alibi for your whereabouts the night your grandfather died."

He took a huge gulp straight from the bottle. "I guess not."

"What can you tell me about the neighbor, Ira Stephens?"

Dwayne rubbed his hands through his oily hair. "Not much. Gramps didn't like him and he didn't like Gramps. When Gramps lived next door, Stephens was always threatening to sue him over anything he could think of. After Gramps moved in with Brent he told me Stephens was going to sue him for allowing all of those kids to mess up the neighborhood."

"Doesn't sound like an amicable relationship to me."

Dwayne started slurring his words, "It wasn't. If you're looking for someone who wanted to kill Gramps, it was probably Stephens."

"I'll go by and visit with Mr. Stephens. Is there anything else you would like to tell me?"

Dwayne set the bottle on the table.

"I didn't kill Gramps. He'd cut me off from borrowing any more from him, but I didn't kill him."

"Thank you for your time, Dwayne. I'll be in touch."

8

HAWK RAPPED ON THE DOOR OF THE WHITE WOOD-
framed house. An elderly man in blue jeans and a red shirt
with stains splattered down the front answered the door.

"Mr. Stephens, may I have a few minutes of your time?
I'm Hawk Theriot. I'm investigating the death of your former
neighbor, Mr. Atkins."

The old man waved his hand.

"C'mon in. I don't know what I can tell you about that old
windbag."

"Thank you. Anything you can share will be helpful.

Stephens pointed Hawk to the tattered sofa.

"You want some coffee? I still have some on from this
morning. It may be a tad strong by now, but that's how I
like it."

"I'd love some."

"I don't have any cream or sugar, so you'll have to drink it
black."

"No problem."

Hawk gazed around the small dusty den while Ira was
retrieving the coffee. He noticed some photographs on the

wall of a much younger Ira Stephenson with an attractive lady accompanying him in almost all of them.

Stephens entered the room.

"My wife. Them's of my wife. Here's your coffee."

"A very attractive lady."

He plopped down in his recliner. "Was. She's been dead for twenty years now."

"Sorry to hear that."

"What do you want?"

Hawk raised his notepad. "I need to fill in a couple of things about Mr. Atkins and the incident the other night."

"Incident, hell. I tried to tell that old coot some of those kids were going to kill him one day if he didn't get a security system for that rundown shack of his."

"We're not sure it was any of the kids, Mr. Stephens."

"Who else could've done it? The only people still using the place after he moved out were those good-for-nothing kids who kept me up all night with their loud music and racket."

"Let's talk about the evening Mr. Atkins died."

Stephens was brusque. "What do you want to know?"

"Did you see anyone in the house earlier in the afternoon?"

"Nope."

"Did you hear anyone around the house before Mr. Atkins arrived?"

"Nope."

"Did you see Mr. Atkins arrive?"

"I saw his light. He couldn't walk straight as old as he was. His light bobbed like a cork on a windy day." Ira laughed at his own comparison.

"You never saw him leave?"

Stephens looked at Hawk, his eyes widening. "Now that's a stupid question. How could he leave if he was dead?"

Hawk glanced back down at his notes.

"I'm just covering the bases. I don't know if he came to the house once or if he left and came back later."

"He didn't come back later." Stephens paused to take a sip of coffee. "He got there a little before ten. I know, because I was getting a drink in the kitchen during the last commercial for the show I was watching and that's when I saw the flashlight."

"How do you know it was Mr. Atkins holding the light?"

"I already told you. He was old and couldn't hold the light steady. I've seen him come and go a bunch of times and it's always the same. I'm surprised he could make it here from his son's house."

"Did you see anyone else go in the house after Mr. Atkins entered?"

Stephens snorted. "Nope."

"Not even Brent?"

"He musta got there while I was having my nightly drink and watching the news. Hey, that's where I've seen you. You were on the news when one of them those guys was killed. I knew I'd seen you somewhere before."

"I was on the local news a couple of times."

"Am I gonna be on television?"

"I doubt it, Mr. Stephens. I'm just helping out the Sheriff with her investigation."

"Oh well." Stephens took another sip of the strong brew. "What else do you want to know about Atkins? I can't tell you I'm sorry he's dead. Now maybe somebody will buy the house and keep all of the riffraff out."

"You didn't like him very much, did you?"

"Nope."

"Why not?"

Stephens sneered, "Because he was a fool, that's why. I can tolerate a lot of things, but being a fool ain't one of 'em."

"What did he do that was so foolish?"

Stephens pointed towards the Atkins house.

"For one, he put up a wood fence on my property?"

"The same one between your property and his now?"

"Yep."

"Why didn't you have him take it down if it's on your property?"

"I tried, but those yahoos down at City Hall agreed with him. They said it was on his property." Stephens threw his free hand up in the air. "I know he paid 'em off to agree with him."

"Was the fence the reason you guys didn't get along well?"

"It was one of them. He used to have his kids and grand-kids and even his great grand-kids over and they'd make all kinds of racket and kept running through my yard. It never quit."

"I take it he never invited you over on these occasions?"

"Nope." Stephens set the empty coffee cup on the table beside the recliner. "Wouldn't have gone anyways. I don't have time for such nonsense."

"For the record, you didn't go to Mr. Atkins's house the night of his murder. Is that correct?"

"Boy, you don't listen. I've already told you I was watching the news and having a drink when those kids killed him."

"Nobody can verify what you're telling me, I suppose."

Stephens stared straight at Hawk.

"Don't need nobody to verify it. I was where I told ya I was."

9

HAWK SAT WITH THE TWINS IN THE CHERRY ROCKING chairs on the back porch of the lodge overlooking the lake.

"You don't know who did it yet?" Mindy couldn't believe it.

Hawk shook his head. "I have a lot of suspects, most of them without alibis, but I can't find anything that points to one particular guy."

Mandy piped up. "Do you want us to help? We're pretty good detectives, you know."

"I know, but you'll be better off if you let me handle this one."

Mindy pleaded. "But we want to help."

"You guys are too involved to be unbiased. You wouldn't be able to focus on the important details."

"So who are the suspects?" Mindy asked.

"Mr. Atkins had three grandsons—"

"Any of them single?" Mandy asked expectantly."

Hawk had to catch up with his thoughts.

"Uh, yeah. One of them is single, but he's not right for one of you."

Mandy poked her lip out.

"You're starting to sound like Dad now. He never thinks any of the guys are right for us. Do all men think like you and Dad when they get old?"

"Hey, I'm not much older than the two of you. I just don't think he's right for one of you."

"Why not?"

"He has some issues."

"And?" Mindy persisted.

"He just has some issues. It wouldn't be good for either of you to get mixed up in those."

"Does that mean he wears pink panties or is mental or what?"

Hawk shook his head. "No, nothing like that. He has some problems he's dealing with."

"Is he sick?"

"He has a gambling and drinking problem. He also has a girl problem."

The twins exchanged confused looks.

Mindy asked. "We understand gambling and drinking, but what's a girl problem?"

"He likes girls."

The twins looked at each other again.

Mindy asked, "And that's a problem?"

Hawk nodded. "It is when you can't remember the girl's name two days later. Look, this is what I mean by focusing on the important details. Now we're off discussing your dating lives and not focusing on the investigation."

"Okay." Mandy said. "But you've got to remember how it was when you were young. Your dating life was important to you, I bet."

She paused.

"Before you met Kristi, I mean."

"Did I hear my name?" Kristie walked onto the back porch.

Hawk looked up with a pleased expression.

"Thank goodness you're here. The twins and I were trying to have a conversation about the investigation, but we didn't get very far. Somehow, we keep getting sidetracked."

Hawk glanced at the twins.

Kristi grinned. "You three getting sidetracked? That's unbelievable. I would've never dreamed."

Hawk shook his head.

"Alright, enough sarcasm. I'm trying to get to the bottom of all of this. What have you found out?"

Kristi sat in the twin rocker next to Hawk.

"Not a whole lot. We found dozens and dozens of fingerprints all over the house. It could take years to run all of them down."

Hawk nodded. "Probably from all the kids going there to look for ghosts."

Mindy protested. "We only went there once."

Mandy supported her twin. "Yeah and look what happened. We didn't even get to see a ghost."

She turned to Mindy.

"I told you we should've gone to the cemetery. We wouldn't have been in as much trouble if we had."

Mindy didn't back down.

"You only wanted to go to the cemetery because Tommy Larson said he might go. I can't help it if you have the hots for him."

"I do not!"

"Yes, you do."

Kristi interrupted the twins. "Hold on girls. We do need to find out what Hawk has uncovered so far."

Mindy didn't take her gaze off her twin.

"Mandy's trying to blame me, but she only wanted to see Tommy. She wasn't interested in meeting a ghost."

"That's not true."

"Girls." Kristi raised her voice. "Can we listen to Hawk for a little while?"

Both of the twins nodded. "Okay."

Hawk's smile never left his face.

"So it isn't just me. For a while, I thought I was going daft."

"You're going daft, but in this case the twins are contributing."

"You said your guys found a lot of prints. Anything else?"

Kristi shook her head.

"Not really. We found footprints, but again they were all sorts of sizes and shapes in the front yard and the back yard. There's no telling how long some of them have been there."

"Anything on the knife?"

"The only prints on it belong to Mindy."

"None from Mr. Atkins?"

"It was clean except for Mindy's."

Hawk rubbed his chin.

"That's odd. I assumed he brought it with him."

"Why?"

"He had a huge collection. Thousands. One of his grandsons also collects knives, but doesn't have nearly as many."

"Maybe we should take a closer look at him. Which one is it?"

"Marshall." Hawk answered. "Marshall has the other collection of knives."

"Did he have a reason to kill his grandfather?"

"He wants his knife collection."

"Does he have an alibi?"

"Not really. He said he was home alone watching TV while his wife and kids were at the movies."

"So he's at the top of the list?"

Hawk shrugged. "We can't rule out his two brothers, or at least one of them."

"Which one?"

"Dwayne."

"What's the story with him?"

"He's the one the twins and I were talking about when we got sidetracked and you showed up."

"Huh?"

"He's single—," Mandy smiled.

"That doesn't make him a murderer," Kristi replied. "If being single makes you a suspect, then we're all on the list."

Mindy popped up. "We were talking about that when we were walking up to the haunted house. You know, you guys not getting married yet. What's the holdup?"

Kristi laughed. Hawk's jaw dropped.

He started stammering, "It's not the right —"

Kristi cut him off. "That is a topic for a different day. Right now, we need to get you girls out of this predicament. Otherwise, how are we going to invite you to the wedding?"

"When is it, Kristi?" Mindy leaned forward expectantly.

Kristi laughed out loud.

"I didn't say we had set a date yet. But let's get back to Dwayne Atkins."

"You have to promise that we'll be bridesmaids."

"I promise. Can we focus on the investigation now?"

"Sure, but go with pastels for the bridesmaids. We look good in pastels."

Hawk shook his head.

"As I was saying, Dwayne is single and has a gambling issue along with that a money-flow issue."

Mandy asked, "What's a money-flow issue?"

"Simply put, there's a lot more money flowing out of his accounts than flowing into them," Hawk replied. "He's broke and was depending on his grandfather to keep bailing him out."

Kristi frowned.

"But if his grandfather was bailing him out, why would he want to kill him?"

"Mr. Atkins recently decided that enough was enough. He was no longer helping Dwayne with his debts. From what I was able to glean, Dwayne's getting some pressure from the people he owes to pay up."

"I imagine the people he owes aren't likely to wait long for their money."

"That's the feeling I get, Kristi."

"Does he have an alibi?"

"Not a good one. He claims he was with a girl, but can't remember her name or even where they met."

"So that's what you meant. No wonder you said he wasn't cut out for us." Mindy sat erect. "We agree with you now that we know the whole story."

"Mandy interjected.

"Hold on, Mindy. Hawk, how much did you say he was going to inherit?"

"I don't know, Mandy," Hawk laughed. "But it's not enough. Until he solves his other problems, he's always going to have money-flow issues."

Mandy looked dejected. "I understand."

Kristi was taking notes. "So we move Marshall from first place on the list and replace him with Dwayne?"

"So far he looks like the one with the most reasons."

"What about the third brother, Brent. He's the one Mr. Atkins was living with. Did you get a chance to talk to him?"

"He has a beautiful home. Looks more like a hotel than a home. Mr. Atkins stayed in a mother-in-law suite segregated from the rest of the house. I guess it was so he could have his own space and Brent and his wife could have some time alone together."

"Doesn't sound like he had any reason to kill his grandfather." Kristi quit taking notes. "He doesn't need the money and he can go buy his own knife collection if he wants one."

"He doesn't want one. He wants to get rid of his grandfather's collection if the will doesn't stipulate who it goes to."

"He's the one also that found the girls at Mr. Atkins house. I don't suppose he could've snuck over there before the twins arrived and done him in?"

"I asked him the very question. He said he tried to tell his wife he was leaving, but she was listening to music in preparation for a solo at church. He didn't think she heard him leave the house from the music room."

"Music room. My oh my. Isn't that special? I wish I had one of those. Not to practice singing, but just to listen to my music. They're soundproof, you know. A lady could get into her own little world in one of those."

"Maybe one day when you get rich and famous."

"I'm willing to settle for the rich part. I'll let the twins have the famous part."

"We'll take it." They said in unison.

"That's okay." Hawk said. "But we don't want you to get famous being found guilty of murder."

Mindy set her jaw and looked Hawk in his eyes.

"We're not gonna be found guilty. We have you and Kristi on our side, so we're not worried about it. Besides, we haven't even gotten married yet. Life isn't over until you get married and have kids. Then we can get found guilty of something."

Hawk and Kristi started to laugh, but then realized the twins were serious for a change.

"We understand." Hawk empathized. "We're gonna do everything we can to find the real killer."

Kristi looked over her notes. "Did you go by the neighbors, a fellow named Stephens?"

Hawk nodded. "Not one of my favorite interviews of all time. Seem like since his wife died, he's not enjoying life a whole lot."

"Did he see anything unusual the night of the murder?"

"He saw Mr. Atkins. At least he's fairly certain it was Atkins. Then he hit the bottle and doesn't remember anything afterward."

"So he's not a suspect in your opinion?"

Hawk shook his head.

"He's an ornery old man without a friend in the world, but I don't believe he is capable of murder. He'd rather complain than act."

"So that leaves us with the three brothers or somebody out of the blue."

Hawk nodded. "That's the size of it."

"Let's put them in some sort of order for further investigation. From what you said, Dwayne has to go to the top of the list because of the money thing."

Hawk nodded.

"Then, I would list Marshall because he wanted to get his hands on the knife collection."

Hawk nodded again.

"Then at the bottom of the list is Brent, whose wife loves music and can't verify when he left the house."

"Yep."

"So what do you want us to do?" Mandy asked.

Kristi stood and addressed both twins. "I know this is hard

on you guys being cooped up like this. But look at it from Hawk's point of view. He's going out of his way to find the truth about the murder and make life easier for both of you at the same time. He's taking time out of his life to help you."

Hawk's eyes widened and he jumped out of his chair. He grabbed Kristi in a huge bear hug.

"Kristi, you're a genius. Have I ever told you that before?"

"Actually, yes."

"Well, you're still a genius. I know who killed Mr. Atkins."

10

THE FUNERAL SERVICE IN THE CHURCH AND THE graveside burial were complete. Hawk squeezed between the well-wishers to get next to Brent.

"Can Kristi and I meet you and your brothers in the church office? We think we know who killed your grandfather."

Brent made no attempt to suppress his surprise. "We'll be right there."

A few minutes later, Brent and his wife, Marshall and his wife and Dwayne all entered the church office to meet with Hawk and Kristi.

"Thank you for coming on short notice." Hawk said to the group.

Dwayne was pacing back and forth. "Can we hurry? The reading of the will is in a couple of hours and we need to make sure we're on time for that."

"Don't worry, Dwayne. Only one of you isn't gonna make it to the meeting."

The brothers all exchanged suspicious glances with each other.

Brent stepped forward. "You said you had some information about the killing. What is it?"

Hawk cast a knowing glance at Kristi. "We know who killed your grandfather."

Brent stepped back. "I know it wasn't me. So that leaves these two."

Marshall almost gasped. "It wasn't me, so it has to be Dwayne."

Dwayne held his hands up.

"I swear. I've done some despicable things in my life, but I didn't kill Gramps. Hawk, you can't pin this on me. It isn't fair."

Brent looked around the room. "Unless you have some solid evidence, I don't see how you're going to charge any of us. Should we get ourselves a lawyer?"

"Wait until I'm finished. Then if you wanta get a lawyer, I'll support you."

Brent looked at Marshall before settling his gaze on Dwayne. "So which one of us do you think is the murderer as if I didn't know?"

Hawk shook his head, "Brent, it isn't Dwayne. He didn't kill your grandfather."

Brent shifted his stare to Marshall. "You? But why?"

Hawk shook his head again. "Brent, it isn't Marshall either."

Brent's eyes widened to their fullest. He was speechless for almost a minute.

"You can't think I did it. I told you I found the girls standing over Gramps."

His voice was much higher than before.

Hawk shook his head for a third time. "No, I know you didn't kill your grandfather."

Brent stood perplexed. "But if it wasn't Dwayne and it wasn't Marshall and you don't think I did it — "

Sarah stood.

"How did you know?" She asked meekly.

Hawk placed a hand on her shoulder. "You told me."

She looked at him with amazement without saying anything.

"You told me it was a shame Mr. Atkins was killed with one of his own knives. The Sheriff's office didn't know whose knife it was and I didn't know. Only the killer knew. Then I realized Brent thought you were in the music room and couldn't provide him with an alibi. He couldn't provide one for you either since he didn't go in the room. You took one of Mr. Atkins knives, snuck out the back door and killed him right before the twins arrived."

Brent faced his wife, almost speechless. "Sarah, why?"

She started sobbing. "Because we were wasting the best years of our lives taking care of him. We could never go anywhere or do anything because we always had to consider him. He could afford the best of care, but chose to make our lives miserable instead."

"Don't say anything else, Sarah. I'll get you the best lawyer in Louisiana."

A female deputy entered the room and handcuffed Sarah Atkins. She led her out of the room followed by the rest of the stunned family.

Kristi turned to Hawk. "What made you think of her?"

"Something you said. It boiled down to the twins being a nuisance and then I remembered that Mr. Atkins had become a huge impediment to Brent and Sarah's lifestyle. So putting two and two together, I came up with Sarah."

Kristi put her arms around Hawk's waist. "We do make a pretty good team together."

"Shh. Don't tell the twins. They'll be trying to set a wedding date for us."

NOTES

Murder at the Haunted House is a short story in the Hawk Theriot & Kristi Blocker series. It features the dynamic duo with even greater challenges.

I have taken great literary license with the geography and data of St. Mary Parish and Morgan City. They are wonderful and a great way to experience the Cajun culture. I lived there for over four years and found it to be one of the most desirable places on earth if you enjoy the outdoors, great cuisine and remarkable people.

There are so many people to thank:

My family, Linda, Josh, Dalton & Jade

David and Sara Sue

C D and Debbie Smith

My brother and sister-in-law, Bill & Pam

My sister, Debbie

My sister-in-law and her husband, Brenda & Jerry

The Sunday School class at Zoar Baptists

Any and all mistakes, typos and errors are my fault and mine alone. If you would like to get in touch with me, go to my web site at http://jimrileyweb.wix.com/jimrileybooks.

I thank you for reading ***Murder at the Haunted House*** and hope you will also enjoy the rest of the series.

Dear reader,

We hope you enjoyed reading *Murder at the Haunted House*. Please take a moment to leave a review, even if it's a short one. Your opinion is important to us.

Discover more books by Jim Riley at

https://www.nextchapter.pub/authors/jim-riley

Want to know when one of our books is free or discounted? Join the newsletter at

http://eepurl.com/bqqB3H

Best regards,

Jim Riley and the Next Chapter Team

You could also like:
Murder in the Cemetery
(Hawk Theriot & Kristi Blocker Short Stories Book 2)

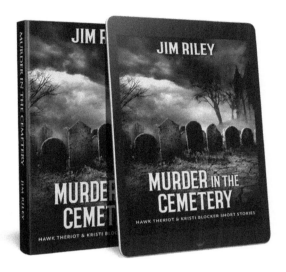

To read the first chapter for free, please head to:
https://www.nextchapter.pub/books/murder-in-the-cemetery

Lightning Source UK Ltd.
Milton Keynes UK
UKHW021900010321
379622UK00012B/1134/J

9 781034 497776